Dawn Flight

a Night Stalkers CSAR romance story
by
M. L. Buchman

Buchman Bookworks

Other works by M.L. Buchman

The Night Stalkers

The Night Is Mine
I Own the Dawn
Daniel's Christmas
Wait Until Dark
Frank's Independence Day
Peter's Christmas
Take Over at Midnight
Light Up the Night
Bring On the Dusk

Firehawks

Pure Heat
Wildfire at Dawn
Full Blaze
Wildfire at Larch Creek
Wildfire on the Skagit

Angelo's Hearth

Where Dreams are Born
Where Dreams Reside
Maria's Christmas Table
Where Dreams Unfold
Where Dreams Are Written

Dieties Anonymous

Cookbook from Hell: Reheated

Saviors 101

Dead Chef

Swap Out!

One Chef!

Two Chef!

SF/F Titles

Nara

Monk's Maze

1

"You gotta be kidding me."

"Do I look like I'm kidding you?"

Captain Jack Slater looked down at the slip of a woman wearing full flight gear but no rank insignia. According to the orders tucked in his pocket, she had the unlikely name of Lois Lang-Clark. Damned cute despite the flight gear that overwhelmed her sleek frame, and the fact that one of her feet was mechanical. Cute despite the *Terminator* foot wasn't a factor though, as she had a ring. Whether it was real or merely to ward off unwanted attention because she was a pretty woman in the man's world of U.S. Army heli-aviation didn't matter. Answer was clearly "no" to all comers, but he couldn't bring himself to leave it totally alone.

"Your husband named Kent?" Maybe this was all some kind of Superman joke? An initiation gag? Army orders weren't big on gags. He looked around the pristine training hangar, but they were the only occupants. No line of guys waiting to laugh when he fell for whatever the newbie game was.

Fresh from two years of Night Stalker school, he'd been on a red-eye flight out of Fort Campbell, Kentucky, landing in the predawn darkness at Joint Base Lewis-McChord in Washington state. He'd stepped out into the cool October morning with first light just cracking the horizon and checked his watch. His orders had sent him straight here in his first hour as a new member of the 160th's 5th Battalion.

But this was a training center.

A line of three flight simulators stood on tall hydraulic pistons that could simulate harsh flight conditions. Each set of pistons supported a white block of metal that looked like nothing so much as a ten-foot-wide white egg on steroids from the outside. He knew from vast experience that the insides looked like very realistic helicopter cockpits, complete with a projection system that could convince you that a crash into downtown Kabul was truly imminent.

After two years he was supposed to be done with this shit.

"Kent Clark?" he nudged when she didn't respond. "Superman in disguise," he prompted and still got back nothing.

With a loud rattle and hiss, the right-most of the simulators, the one for the MH-47G Chinook heavy lift helo, bucked and slewed hard left. By the sustained nose down attitude, he could tell that its pilot was not having a good day. The left hand one for the MH-6 Little Bird was in a slow, steady climb. The one in the middle, the one for his baby, the MH-60M Black Hawk, stood quietly at rest. Waiting.

"My husband's name is Kendall," the slim woman informed him in a tone as warm as an iceberg. "Kendall Clark."

He laughed, he couldn't help himself. A crazy name, a ring, and a false foot. What the hell? Could she even fly with that thing?

Her silence was more deafening than the two simulators, now both protesting loudly as they jerked and twisted.

"I'm already FMQ. Fully Mission Qualified," Jack explained and had the sudden feeling that he was being more rather than less of an idiot with each passing moment. He rubbed at his face trying for a reset. "Look I need some sleep. Can you point me in the right direction and we'll play out your little game later?"

"You signed up for Combat Search and Rescue?"

"Damn straight!" Bringing out the wounded from a hot battle zone was the kind of serious-as-shit job he'd always dreamed of. One he'd been gunning for since the moment he'd learned it existed. He liked the idea of rescuing people who really needed it. It fit something right in his brain.

"If you haven't been signed off by me, then you aren't Fully Mission Qualified for CSAR activities with the 5th Battalion. Period."

Jack thought of several short sharp comebacks. But there was something in her tone that gave him pause.

One of the simulators slammed to a halt, tipped at a hard angle against the stops. Then, with a groan, it eased and lowered into the reset position.

At that moment, two other people joined them.

One climbed down from the Black Hawk simulator, a grizzled, gray-hair with faded Master Sergeant stripes on his uniform—those took a long time to fade. He came to a parade rest close behind Superman's wife. That said that just maybe she was for real and it was time he started listening.

The second was a tall brunette who'd come in the same hangar door he had. Even had a big duffle, worn pack-fashion over nice strong shoulders. Now that was his idea of a woman. Eyes as dark as her hair, a fine face wearing an easy smile, and almost as tall as he was.

"Excuse me." Voice smooth and low. Unlike Mrs. Superman, her flight gear didn't overwhelm her frame.

"Yes?" he replied before Superwoman could speak.

The new arrival looked him up and down, "I'm guessing you're not Major Lois Lang-Clark unless your parents hated you when they named you."

There might have been a twitch of a smile; or there might have been a roast-in-hell-macho-asshole look. Jack was too tired to tell. *Major* Lang-Clark? He'd forgotten that from his orders. He'd just been dumb enough to be harassing a major? Bad start for first day in a new battalion.

"You want Mrs. Superman, here," he pointed to the slender figure still glaring up at him.

The new arrival turned and saluted sharply, "Captain Diana Price reporting."

Again, the laugh burst from him. He just couldn't stop it though he knew he was only digging his grave deeper.

The Master Sergeant and the two women turned to look at him.

"I'm sorry," Jack did his best to sober at their bland expressions. "Mrs. Superman Lois Lang-Clark meets Diana Price. You probably don't know, no sane person would, but Diana *Prince* was the secret identity of Wonder Woman. It's just too damned funny."

The tall brunette turned so that he could see the helmet dangling off the other side of her duffle bag. On the side was painted a wide golden triangle with a red star at the center, curved like the heroine's headband. Below that was the stylized "WW" that arced across the breasts of Wonder Woman's comic book uniform.

The petite instructor held out the helmet she had tucked under her arm. On it was emblazoned the Superman logo.

He held up both his hands in hopeless resignation.

The women didn't look amused and he almost kept it in.

But then he caught the merry twinkle in the gray-haired Master Sergeant's eye and Jack totally lost it.

2

Some men did not deserve to live and Diana had just met a prime example. Big, handsome, and a total jerk. Of course, after a decade as an Army aviator and Black Hawk pilot, she should be used to dealing with that by now.

It was the great laugh that was throwing her. Macho jerks weren't supposed to have laughs that made you want to smile right along with them.

But it wasn't that hard to resist, especially looking at Major Lang-Clark's serious expression.

"Why are you flying CSAR?" the Major ignored the buffoon's attempts to recover.

How many times had she been asked that? Always by men who were testing, pushing, looking for that weakness that would say she was the wrong person for the role. It wasn't sexual bias, at least not all of the time. Many of the examiners were equally stringent about men applying for CSAR, because this wasn't the Gulf War Army of her mother's day.

Still, it was the first time a woman had ever asked her the question. Diana would prefer not to answer in front of Mr. Jerk, but she'd been asked, so she'd reply, with something other than the "Want to serve and save people" line.

"My father died in Kuwait during Desert Storm. Before they knew about the Golden Hour or had the systems in place to take advantage of it."

Modern CSAR was now all about recovering casualties and getting them into a hospital within one hour—with faster being much better. For severe bleeding, sixty minutes was the line of near hundred percent fatality. Thirty minutes marked a fifty percent survival rate, and all but the very worst cases could be kept alive for fifteen minutes.

A CSAR pilot's job was to deliver the medics within that quarter hour if possible, and get the casualty to the hospital inside the hour no matter what hell was breaking loose.

Her father had hung on for two-and-a-half hours in the Kuwaiti Desert, but there hadn't been the assets in place to get to him sooner. Medical help other than his squad mates' first-aid had arrived too late. That her mother had been an unmarried and, she'd soon discovered, pregnant supply sergeant, had denied her both her own military benefits and her sworn fiancé's death benefits.

"If I can save one person who is somebody's father, I want to be the one doing it," Diana's voice had gone harsh. She closed her eyes for a moment and when she swallowed hard, it hurt.

A comforting hand rested on her shoulder. To her surprise, when she opened

her eyes it belonged to the laughing jerk—
except now his expression was sober and
sympathetic. Maybe there was a person
inside there…though she wasn't willing to
bet on it.

3

Jack was pointed to the copilot's seat. Well, he supposed that he'd earned that, though it rankled.

Diana the Wonder Woman had been sent to their simulator's right-side pilot-in-command seat.

The Major sat in a jump seat close behind them. Master Sergeant Hamlin had settled in the chair that would control the simulator experience.

Jack settled himself in for a couple hours of boredom. Start-up, take-off, basic flight… After five years with the 10th

Mountain's Combat Aviation Brigade and two more years of Night Stalker training, you'd think he could skip all this basic crap. But nooo.

Shit.

However, knowing he had ground to make up with the Major, he settled in to do what he did best, fly.

Captain Diana Price started out with an attitude of sharp competence. She adjusted the seat and safety harness with the motions of long familiarity. He'd never flown with a woman, but she showed the signs of a skilled pilot, so he'd give her the benefit of the doubt until she had a chance to prove herself.

And there was no doubt about her commitment—not by how her voice and face had shifted. No matter how much of a showpiece she might look on the outside, she cared deeply about CSAR on the inside, and with good reason. He wished his reasons were so clear. They were just as strong, somehow, but he'd never been able to sort them out into words. Another point in Wonder Woman's favor.

"Ready?" Major Lang-Clark asked over the simulator's intercom.

Jack made one last visual inspection. The side-by-side pilots seats were separated by a wide bank of radio and navigation gear. That swept up into a broad, sideways dashboard that crossed in front of them and ended about chest high. On the console were six large glass screens, each the size of a tablet computer. The simulator was rigged just like the latest glass-cockpit standard which was nice—once he'd gotten used to the digital cockpit, going back to the old analog dials and gauges was always frustrating.

A couple arm's lengths beyond the outside of the windshield was the blank screen on which would be projected their "view" during the simulated flight. Additional viewports to the Earth below were down under the console beside where his feet rested on the rudder pedals.

Collective under his left hand to control lift, and cyclic joystick rising between his legs for his right hand to control direction and speed of flight. Both controls were studded with a dozen buttons and switches. He brushed his fingers over them, now so familiar with practice that he knew them as well as he did where his nose was on his face.

He saw Diana doing the same, confirming that the unfamiliar simulator was indeed familiar. Their matching sets of controls meant that between them, they'd always have control of the aircraft, even if one or the other had to reach out to adjust something on the dash or radios.

He pulled down his helmet's semi-transparent visor and double-checked that the head's up display calibration was properly projected across the inside surface.

"Ready," he and Diane spoke in almost perfect unison.

"Good. Let's go."

The goddamn simulator exploded.

4

Diana's instincts took over before she could make sense of the transition.

One moment she'd been preparing to show the Major that she did indeed have the basics down solid—she'd had to prove herself so many times over the last decade that the rote routines were almost comforting with their familiarity.

The next moment, she was diving left as the audio warning system squealed in her right ear identifying an incoming attack of small caliber rifle fire from that side and the computer was showing targeting data.

Before she could call out to Jack the Jerk, he'd nudged the cyclic just enough to shift the aim of the weapons mounted on the outside of the helo. He launched a pair of Hydra 70 rockets; their simulated streaks raced right down onto the origin point of the ground fire.

He was back off the cyclic an instant later.

Jack had integrated into the simulation so fast that he must have known what was coming. Maybe he was another trainer, had to be with the way he'd been sparring with the Major. "Mrs. Superman" indeed; as if Superwoman didn't deserve her own name.

A battle raged overhead…and they weren't really a part of it. Three Black Hawks and a pair of Little Birds were dodging and diving over a convoy at the far end of the narrow valley.

"*CSAR 01*. Two wounded, grid thirty-nine," the Major's voice informed her with the dispassion of a mission commander sitting in some distant command bunker.

A blink to shift her focus from inside her visor to glance down at the electronic map on the console. Grid thirty-nine was right at the heart of the battle.

"Do it!" Captain Jack Slater snarled.

"Roger that!" Diana yanked up the collective and shoved the cyclic forward. She dove hard and fast down into the throat of the valley. A dozen targets presented themselves.

She started to turn for one, when the Major shouted, "Someone else's problem. Get the wounded. That's always your priority."

Gritting her teeth, Diana flew through a rain of small fire, bullets too light to penetrate the Black Hawk's armor…hopefully.

She swooped and settled into Grid 39.

"Medics away," the Master Sergeant reported.

She sat interminably—the mission clock counted ten, twenty, thirty seconds—wincing every time a round pinged off her windshield with a bright *Thwack!*

"Ten," Sergeant Hamlin called out.

Instinct had her looking to the side port to watch for the medics only ten seconds out. All she could see was the swirling brownout that would have been caused by her own helo's rotors stirring up the dust and dirt…if this was real.

"Raising to hover," Jack eased up on the copilot controls and hers moved with him.

Damn it. She should have thought of that. It would save them several seconds in getting the hell out of here if they were at a ground-hugging hover by the time the medics boarded.

"Four aboard," Sergeant Hamlin announced.

And just as she was about to lift he called out again.

"Still missing a medic."

"We're what?"

In answer, a wounded soldier hobbled out of the brownout, moving slowly toward her. Assisting him was a young woman dressed like a CSAR medic.

And a dozen meters to their left a battered pickup swung into view through the dust cloud. The "technical" had an out-sized machine gun mounted on the truck bed.

Its first salvo star-cracked her windscreen.

This wasn't the small rifle fire of before; this was .50 cal machine gun fire that would chew them apart in seconds.

Time to go. Now!

She couldn't leave the two injured.

Her helo wouldn't survive if she hesitated.

But she did.

The last sound she was aware of was a soft but heart-felt, "Holy shit!" from Jack Slater.

5

Then the simulation ended like a switch thrown and Jack slammed forward against his safety harness into the sudden void left by the end of the projection. He eased back into his seat and flexed his fingers trying to get his hands to stop shaking. He blinked out the helo's windows, now the bland light gray of an empty projection screen wrapped around the simulator's cabin.

No sign of the shattered windscreen.

Or the bad guys.

Or the wounded.

The silence was deafening.

With fumbling fingers he managed to find the chin strap of his helmet and pull it free.

He looked over at Diana, but she looked little better off. Sweat streamed down her face and her eyes were wide with shock.

"We were in the simulation for…" he couldn't even finish the question his throat was so dry.

"Sixty seconds. Maybe."

He rubbed at his face, "Felt like a goddamn week."

"It did," she sighed and slumped in her seat.

There was a strange, asymmetrical clumping that sounded like someone with two different…

Major Lang-Clark stepped into view outside the window, between the simulator's cabin and the projection screen. Right, the woman had one real foot and one artificial one. Clearly not a factor. She was a pure hard-ass about Combat Search and Rescue and nothing else mattered. He was sure he'd have no trouble remembering that detail in the future.

"CSAR Training," she said as she looked in at the two of them. "Begins tomorrow at 0700. Get some sleep."

She began walking back out of view, but stopped and looked at them over her shoulder.

If he didn't know better, he'd say her smile was almost kindly.

"The decisions," her voice was soft, without the hard edge she'd used since the moment of his less-than-respectful arrival, "get harder from here." Then she was gone.

Jack's groan was cut off when a strong hand clapped down hard on his shoulder from behind.

He looked up at the Master Sergeant.

"She's a pistol, ain't she?" Then he shook Jack like a ragdoll, before heading toward the ladder while whistling *The Army Goes Rolling Along* happily to himself.

"You okay?" he asked Diana.

Diana nodded once, uncertainly. Then again with a little more surety.

"Don't beat on yourself. Even Wonder Woman couldn't have gotten out of that."

"But in real world, what would you do?"

He thought about the situation again: escape, make that *possible* escape, but only at the price of committing others to death including their own medic.

"You don't know, do you?" she wasn't being nasty. It sounded as if she really hoped he did.

"Damned if I do," he hated letting her down. "Maybe Major Mrs. Superman will let us know, if we behave."

"I wouldn't bet on it. Lesson for the student and all that crap."

He like her attitude and her easy confidence. "How about if I buy you breakfast at the Mess Hall and we can discuss it a bit?" It wasn't that he wanted to share a meal with such a fine-looking woman...well, he did, but it wasn't just that. For perhaps the first time in his career, he was well and truly stumped. Flying always just came easy to him, but this was hard.

She nodded, shook her head, then nodded again.

He couldn't tell if she'd heard or even understood him.

She covered her face with her hands for a moment and gave a small scream of frustration that almost made him feel like smiling again. Then she pulled her hands away and turned to face him.

"It depends," between one moment and the next she'd gotten her act back together. Just that fast. Which was pretty damned amazing.

He wasn't even close to having his own act back together after that simulation. "Depends on what?"

"Are you always a jerk?"

Jack grinned at her, "Depends on who you ask. A couple commanders, several ex-girlfriends, Mom…more like a pain in the ass."

"A pain in the ass is better than a jerk?" She shrugged. "Well, I always preferred forming my own opinions."

6

Breakfast almost lapsed into lunch.

Not jerk, Diana assessed. Too sure of himself perhaps, though he sounded as if he had some reason to be.

Well, if he did, so did she. They'd both made it through the notoriously difficult selection process of the Army's 160th Special Operations Aviation Regiment, and nobody in any military had more skilled helicopter pilots than the Night Stalkers of SOAR.

And they'd both volunteered to go CSAR, which took a special kind of masochism—

flying into hot battle zones to extract the wounded rather than fighting from far above until the battle was done and won.

While Jack Slater didn't tell her why he'd gone CSAR, she was finding it easier and easier to like the man. He always found the lighter side—he was funny. Not like one of those guys who only thought he was funny, but one that actually was.

The emblem on the side of his helmet was an impossibly elaborate sword. When she finally asked if he was King Arthur, he'd told her she was really close, but kept her guessing for a while. She finally gave up.

"Jack. Jack Slater," he said it like "Bond. James Bond."

"Your name," she'd replied still not getting it.

He'd practically chortled with delight. "Jack Slater. Jack Slaughter. Jack the Killer. Jack the Giant Killer. They had me pegged by the end of first formation at West Point. King Arthur was the original of the Giant Killer myths; Jack came along a handful of centuries later. You see, you might be a fictional heroine, but I'm mythic! And I'll put my magic sword up against your golden lasso anytime."

Mythic or not, he was sharp. They dissected that morning's mission at length and finally decided they should have gone for the escape. Once clear, there were more options: to return, to send in others. But to sit still was to kill them all.

They pounded out possible counter tactics for the future. Drop off the medics and automatically return to the sky to await their return? Too much risk of having to abandon the team.

Stay just inches aloft? Tricky to sustain and it would continue to stir dust badly, perhaps making it harder for the medics to recover the injured, but offering far more flexibility in an attack scenario.

Jack made a couple of forays at finding out more about her past, but she just couldn't go there. It was too deep and she was still shocked that she had blurted it out, even that one little part.

And refusing to go there, she couldn't ask about his past.

But he'd been kind enough to stay backed away rather than pushing or wheedling as any other guy would have.

By the time they tracked down their apartments in the on-site barracks they were both weaving with exhaustion. They were on the same floor of the same unit. There were definite advantages to being an officer in an elite outfit—no open barracks. They stood close in the dimly lit common hall. It was barely big enough to hold a stairwell, the doors to four tiny one-bedroom apartments, and both of them with their duffle bags.

They stood in that little hall, too close together, but she found herself reluctant to move away. She'd only flown in from Hunter Army Airfield this morning, so it's not as if she knew this place. The only thing she did know was Captain Jack "the Giant Killer" Slater.

"Are you sure you're not a jerk?"

"You mean despite my demonstration with Major Mrs. Superman this morning?"

"Despite that," she didn't even know what she was asking.

"Well," he aimed that powerful smile of his at her again, "will it make me more of a jerk if I do what I want, or what I should?"

"Hard to know because I don't know what the hell you're talking about soldier." Unless, maybe she did.

"Am I more of a jerk if I kiss you like I've been wanting to since the moment you showed me that screwy Wonder Woman helmet of yours?"

She definitely knew what he was talking about.

"Or is it worse if I don't kiss you and walk away as if you aren't beautiful, desirable, great company, and a hell of a pilot?"

It had to be lack of sleep talking, but what the hell. "I think the latter would make you much, much more of a jerk." No other man had ever thought to include how she flew in a string of compliments. That last was the scale tipper.

He looked at her with some surprise.

"Well?" Now that she'd said it, she did want him to kiss her, preferably before she decided just how stupid an idea that might be.

Jack shrugged his duffle bag off his shoulder and it thudded onto the floor. With an easy strength, he lifted the strap of hers off her shoulder and lowered it as well.

Then, with a gentleness she hadn't expected, he pulled her into his arms, offering her a dozen opportunities to escape or evade.

When she failed to vary the course of his approach, he completed the gesture. It wasn't just some kiss, some hand around her neck and a fiery meeting of the lips and tongue.

Kissing Jack Slater included a full body hug as if they'd been lovers for years. His arms wrapped naturally around her, as hers slid up his chest and around his neck.

He tasted of the ice cream dessert they'd just split, the strawberries that he'd chosen and the chocolate sauce that she had. And he felt soldier hard and magnificent.

This wasn't her mother's war. She didn't want a child from a dead man that would ruin her career.

For that reason, she'd sworn off military men.

Until this moment.

For tonight, at least, this wasn't her mother's Army either.

She led Jack Slater into her new apartment.

7

Jack woke up tangled in sheets and woman.
It was pitch dark and a helicopter had just
roared by close overhead. Then another
followed it—and several more.

"Two Black Hawks, four Chinooks,"
the woman in his arms whispered. Wonder
Woman. And Diana had certainly proved
several times last night that she completely
deserved the accolade.

"Plus a pair of Little Birds and a partridge
in a pear tree," he replied. "You know that
a woman who can tell helo models by their
sound is pretty sexy."

She nuzzled his neck. "Gods, I feel like such a slut."

"I've been used," he groaned in mock complaint. He slid a hand down over that fine soldier's butt of hers, the other tracing over that long leg of hers draped across his waist. "However, I would point out that no way does a slut feel this good."

"You say the sweetest things."

"I'm a sweet guy."

She snorted against his neck, her laugh sending interesting ripples along where their bodies lay together.

"Okay," he admitted. "You caught me," and he wiggled a finger in the ticklish spot he'd located earlier, the soft inside of her thigh just above the knee.

She convulsed and he used her momentary imbalance to leverage her back under him.

He groped for some more protection and she didn't make a single protest as he did his best to prove that he wasn't sweet at all.

8

Simulator scenarios were mixed with actual night flights. And as one flight turned into a dozen, then two dozen, so did their days together—for daytime is when Night Stalkers slept, or didn't.

Diana was going weak in her head for a fellow officer which was stupid in so many ways. It would help if he wasn't such a joy to fly with or an equal joy to tussle with between the sheets—but he was both of those and more.

In a blur so fast that it was hard to imagine, a cold October dawn had turned

into a bitter December, but she didn't care.
The training regimen from Major Lang-
Clark was intense—and serving its purpose.
The confusion of that first simulation had
turned into a clear set of skills, even if the
new simulations posed even harder moral
dilemmas and more difficult to perfect tactics.

And Captain Jack Slater had turned
into the best man she'd ever been with.
She simply couldn't get enough of him, no
matter how much they both tried.

They alternated seats, both in the simulator and aloft until one night he looked
at her after a particularly complex storm-
and-mountain scenario and declared, "You
should be pilot-in-command from now on.
You're better than I am."

"No way. You're—" then she saw Major
Lang-Clark and Sergeant Hamlin nodding
in agreement.

"You two," Lois spoke, "make an interesting team in several ways. I've met better," she tapped her own chest in a rare jest,
"but I haven't trained better. We normally
would split you up after training, send you
out with different units."

And the breath had caught in Diana's throat. She and Jack had been together only a few months and already she couldn't imagine *not* waking up to Jack's hard body and gentle teasing. Or flying with anyone else. They'd developed a synchronicity in the air that was as effortless as their one on the ground.

"But," Lois continued, "keep on the way you are and I'll recommend you remain teamed up."

Lois' look carried a second meaning that Diana wanted to be surprised by, but wasn't. They'd done their best to keep their relationship behind the closed apartment door, but obviously that hadn't worked.

"Of course, long-term planning in these situations is always an interesting challenge," and Lois left them, shooing the Sergeant out of the simulator ahead of her.

Only when the cockpit was quiet, all of the systems dark and dormant, and the last echoes of the others' footsteps down the ladder had long since died away, did she dare turn to look at Jack.

He wasn't looking at her.

He was staring straight ahead, out at the blank screen, with his hands still clenched hard on the controls.

"Jack?"

9

Jack had had plenty of other lovers like Diana Price.

He was sure he had.

Oh, maybe not as smart. Or quite as pretty. Or so goddamn amazing in bed. Or such a good pilot he'd finally had to face his own shortcomings—but he was a better gunner and navigator than she was and that had to count for something.

But all those others had been just like her in…no way he could seem to recall. What the hell?

"Jack?"

He heard her voice, distant, worried. He wanted to brush it off. Toss out some Jack-the-Giant-Slaughter joke that had always cracked up the guys, eased any situation.

But a panic had coursed through him that he didn't know how to handle.

"Jack?" This time the voice was worried, afraid. Anyone else he could ignore, any woman but Diana.

He forced his attention to her.

Her eyes were pleading with him, wanting to understand something he couldn't grasp, a past even Jack-the-Giant-Slayer couldn't kill.

"I—" he tried and failed. So he started again. "I *am* a jerk."

She blinked at him in surprise.

"I'm not a permanent sort of guy. No one has ever been dumb enough to think that I was. Especially not me."

He could see the pain slam into her as if he'd gut-punched her, hard.

"Diana. You're a wondrous woman. You're way too smart to think that I'm more than I am." But the pain in her eyes grew worse, darker. "Aren't you?"

Tears spilled over and flowed freely down her cheeks.

One moment she was there, her tears leaving him totally helpless. The next she was racing out of the simulator.

He slammed against the harness in his effort to follow her and knocked most of the wind out of himself. Slapping the releases, he dumped his helmet—still wired into the simulator's systems—and ran after her.

She was fast, but he was faster. He caught her out on the airfield close beside a parked Black Hawk helicopter, barely visible as any hint of dawn was lost beneath the thickly overcast night.

He grabbed her and the slap came fast and hard. Enough to jerk his head aside and fill the night sky with stars.

Jack released his hold and she was gone again.

10

Jack had never slept in his own apartment.
He rubbed his own eyes groggily. Well,
his record was unbroken. He'd lain awake
through the whole day, aware of Diana
lying only a few feet away on the other side
of the wall between their apartments.

At times he imagined he could hear her
weeping, at times he'd imagined that he
was.

Half a dozen times he'd crossed the tiny
hall to knock on her door, but not knowing
what to say, he'd crept silently back to his
own room each time.

On his last try, his packed duffle bag fell into the apartment when he'd opened his door; she'd packed his gear and left it leaning there. He hadn't the heart to try and cross the vast divide of the small hallway after that.

"You really are a jerk," he told his reflection as he shaved.

At least his reflection wasn't answering back.

"Permanent is a lie," he continued. His parents and numerous stepparents on both sides of the house had proved that time and again. He had no brother or sister, but he had step-ones right and left. And then ex-stepparents were breeding more kin, many of whom he'd never met or maybe never even heard of. They should start holding extended-family reunions, so that there could be more excuses for divorces and marriages among the ever expanding catastrophe that was his family. Maybe they had; he certainly wasn't in touch with any of them.

He finished shaving and inspected himself in the mirror. He should have left the five p.m. shadow; clean-shaven, Diana's palm print stood out clearly. Well, maybe not enough for anyone else to notice it, but he could see and feel every line, right down to the whorls of her fingerprints.

If ever there was a woman who deserved permanent, it was Diana Price.

He wished it could be him, but it just wasn't going to happen.

But he wished it could.

He got dressed in whatever he found first. Most of his clothes were a jumble, stuffed down into the duffle. At least Diana hadn't slashed them.

Had he been leading her on? Making promises he had no intention or ability to keep? No.

Had his body been making promises he couldn't keep? He was less comfortable with that answer.

It was a night off. He hid in the base library like the coward that he was. Not that he understood a word he read. He'd never met anyone like Diana Price the Wonder Woman and had never expected to again.

So what was he going to do about it?

Even if he wanted to do something about it, would she let him?

Not if she was smart. Which she was.

His stomach growled for the third meal after he'd skipped the first two; the traitor.

He still had no answers when he saw her eating on the far side of the mess hall from their usual place.

Nor when the PA system called out their names halfway through the meal to report immediately to the flight line.

11

The weather sucked! Which was fine, it completely fit Diana's equally foul mood. While she hadn't slept, the first major winter storm had arrived and high winds were now slashing driving sheets of rain across the base. Trees were down throughout Puget Sound. The Nisqually and Puyallup Rivers already racing toward flood stage.

The television, her only friend through the sleepless night, told the story of massive power outages sweeping far and wide across the Pacific Northwest, though none had hit Joint Base Lewis-McChord.

A hundred times through the day she'd thought how nice it would be to curl up with Jack Slater, make love while the wind roared and the rain battered—and a hundred times she'd had to push it aside.

Late within the time she was supposed to be asleep, about three in the afternoon because they were now fully on a night-time schedule like most Night Stalkers, she'd finally forced herself to start thinking.

Why had she reacted so strongly?

Because just like her mother—who had never remarried and maybe at long last Diana understood why—she'd fallen in love.

Diana had sighed and wished she wasn't always so goddamn honest with herself. But it was true. Without even noticing, she'd fallen in love with Jack Slater.

But Jack had made no promises.

He'd always been appreciative: of her flying, her mind, and her body. He had an uncanny ability to fully focus on each aspect of her. When they were discussing a mission, he wasn't leering at her body, he was a hundred percent on profile. And when they were making love…he made the rest of the world cease to exist.

Except for her initial info dump about her father's death, they'd never discussed their pasts, not even that she was illegitimate. Past missions, training, even schooling, sure. But there'd been a barrier when they got back to family that neither of them had been willing to breach.

Well, the three-minute trip in the back of the SUV that raced them across the airfield was not the time to discuss it.

That was the moment when Diana decided that she wasn't ready to give up on them yet.

She wanted Jack. She wanted him long-term. He was already in her heart the same way that her father was in Mom's.

Forever.

A hundred yards to the hangar, she did the only thing there was time for; the only thing she could think to do.

She reached out and took his hand.

He didn't turn to look at her, didn't react in any way.

Except to nearly crush her fingers in his powerful grip. He held on like a drowning man for every single one of those seconds.

She'd take that as a good sign.

12

"Dungeness Spit lighthouse," **Lois** shouted at them over the roar of the storm. "It's out on a sand spit in the middle of the Strait of San Juan de Fuca. All of the Coast Guard helos are scrambling on emergencies out in the shipping lanes. No way to get a boat out there quickly and they've passed the call to us. Civilian caretaker, heart attack. His wife radioed it in."

Without a word, he and Diana had prepped the Black Hawk. A base medic and Master Sergeant Hamlin piled aboard.

"What about you?" he asked the Major.

She shook her head.

She'd never told her story, but she was a damn fine pilot with or without two real feet. And she was perhaps the tactically smartest person he'd ever met, definitely about CSAR. There was only one other woman he'd want beside him more.

Again the Major refused. "I don't fly enough myself to have the needed edge. And if I go and can't fly, I'd just make everyone crazy."

She made it sound funny, but the pain on her rain-soaked face was enough to send him clambering aboard, because he knew it would be even worse if he said even another word. She gave so much, but she'd lost a lot too.

Less than three minutes later they were hammering aloft. Usually the hazards were man-made when he flew: bullets, RPGs, missiles. Tonight was much rougher, the storm slashing in from the Pacific was ripped apart by the tall mountains of the Olympic Peninsula then recombined in harsh and unpredictable ways.

There was no time to talk. Eighty miles should be an easy twenty-minute flight, instead it was a nightmare of blacked-out chaos, battering winds, tall mountains, and numerous aircraft corridors for the four major airports from here to Everett—the last requiring careful navigation to avoid being eaten by a hundred tons of airline. It took everything they could muster to get through the storm.

Some of the gusts were fully half the speed they were able to fly. And the wind came from all different directions, including vertical. They'd jump from ten thousand feet to twelve and then fall back to eight faster than he could recite the nursery rhyme to remind himself, "Jack be nimble."

If the flight out was bad, the approach to Dungeness Spit off Sequim, Washington was insane.

The Strait was a twenty-mile wide pipe-line aimed right at the heart of the storm.

Sequim was blacked out, of course, except for anyone with a generator.

Five miles offshore, the lighthouse was a bright beacon, which only made it all the more visible how their helo was being battered about the sky.

Whole sections of the thin spit of sand that connected the mainland to the lighthouse were being swept by towering waves. He turned on the landing spotlight and they could see drift logs a hundred feet long being tossed about like a game of pickup sticks.

He monitored the engine and navigation data, and kept his hands on the controls to help when needed.

"God but you're good, Wonder Woman," he told her over the intercom. Why he hadn't said a word until they were approaching the worst part of the flight was beyond him. That simple hand clasp had given him something incredible. It had given him hope. He wasn't sure yet hope for what, but it had flooded through him and it was a feeling he didn't want to lose ever again.

"Thanks," he could hear how tight she was holding on, how hard she was working.

"Take a breath, Diana."

She exhaled out hard, then again.

"Been holding your breath for the whole flight?"

"Maybe," some warmth came back into her voice. "We Wonder Women can do that."

"Haven't found a thing you can't do yet."

13

Diana could. She couldn't win the heart
of Jack Slater. And she didn't know why.
After she'd exposed herself in the car by
taking his hand, he hadn't said a single word
to her that wasn't calling out a flight vector
or an engine status.

At least now he was talking.

Right when she couldn't; she had to
concentrate.

The lighthouse itself sat in a broad
meadow that rose barely above sea level. The
lighthouse and keeper's cottage crouched
at the center of the meadow a hundred

meters from the ocean to both the north and south, but if its elevation was five meters, she'd be surprised. Huge logs had been washed up close to the lighthouse to either side.

There was a helipad, and it was awash. It was also too far from the caretaker's cottage. But she didn't dare get too close either or she might catch a rotor blade.

Everything else faded into the background, storm, waves, even Jack. There was only her and her target. The MH-60M Black Hawk had become merely an extension of her will, as much a part of her as the clothes she wore.

She fought her way down, a side gust almost flipping her over, but she wrenched the helo back aloft, missed the lighthouse by mere feet over a rotor's diameter—far closer than she'd meant to come—and tried again.

She had the feel of the gusts. How each massive wave, rising to attack the seaward shore, momentarily blocked the rush of the wind right at ground level.

Finally there was a moment…

"Hang on!" Diana shouted over the intercom and used one of the unusual capabilities of the Black Hawk, its impressive ability to survive a crash.

From five meters up and driving ahead hard into the wind, she slammed the collective down and yanked back on the cyclic.

The Black Hawk fell like a brick. The rear wheel hit first, then, like a belly flop, the helicopter hammered down on her main wheels. Diana was slammed down into her seat, but they were designed to take it, even if it didn't feel like it at the moment. Her teeth clacked together hard.

The helo bounced, but not high. That's why Diana had slammed down the collective. The Black Hawk was now pinned to the ground by the rotor blades still trying to descend even though they were on the blowing grass of the meadow.

"Beware the low rotors!" The attitude of the blades would be sucking their tips closer to the ground than was normal for a Black Hawk, from eight feet to perhaps six.

Sergeant Hamlin yanked open the big cargo bay just as a big gust slammed into them. Moisture, air thick with salt, and cold assaulted her.

She heard a cry and a foul, "Damn it!" from the medic.

"What?" She twisted around but couldn't see anything.

"Hold on," it was Hamlin and he grunted as he spoke.

Diana watched the mission clock count out five seconds and was about to repeat her shout when Hamlin spoke again.

"Doc stepped out and caught the bad gust. Think he broke his ankle."

"Shit, sorry!" The medic's voice came back on the intercom, wrenched in pain. "Maybe a sprain, but I don't think I can walk on it."

"I got this," Jack laid his hand over hers on the collective for a moment and squeezed her fingers. He mouthed something else she couldn't see in the darkness; damn him!

He opened the copilot door and there was a great flurry. With an open passage now completely through the helo, the wind grabbed anything that had been left loose in the cargo bay and ripped it out the copilot's door, all of the detritus battering at Jack. Under the barrage, he rolled out on the gust and then fought his door closed. Ducking low around the nose, he raced around to grab the other end of the stretcher that Hamlin was wrestling with.

She watched Jack and Hamlin disappear into the storm, then reset the mission clock and began watching it count the seconds. The medic lay in back, thumping around and cursing for all the good it did anyone.

Outside the windscreen, the wind was heaving miscellaneous detritus across the low island. Waves were tossing logs ashore. Smaller pieces that broke off tumbled along the ground. The helo's bright landing light showed each wave that lifted, far taller than the Black Hawk. Then it crashed down on the beach so much closer than she was comfortable with.

"Hurry, goddamn it!" she shouted to no one in particular.

The lighthouse's beam, shining from twenty meters above their heads, caught the hint of something other than water moving in its far-reaching light. She waited for it to sweep around and cast its light on the nightmare scene once more.

"I'm sure they're—" the medic started.

The light swung to light the waves once more and—

"Hang on!" Diana shouted and yanked up on the collective. It wasn't even a thought, it was now trained into pure instinct. She was aloft by the time a dinghy had tumbled from the waves and crossed her previous position. The little boat was snarled in a fishing net that was floating up and billowing on the wind as if it were an evil ghost net hoping to ensnare her. If even an edge of it snagged the rotor, it would bring the Black Hawk down hard.

She cleared it by mere feet.

More detritus passed by: plastic barrels, those big orange boat bumpers, another dinghy. There was a boat in real trouble out there.

She shouldn't be flying without a co-pilot, but she didn't have a whole lot of choice. And riding this weather alone was the hardest thing she'd ever done.

"Damn you twice, Jack Slater."

Not daring to land yet, Diana eased forward into the storm, but found no big fishing boat battered in the surf.

"Hey! Where are you?" a shout came over the radio.

"Coming back to you," she called over the radio. "Stay by the lighthouse until I'm in."

She repeated her crash landing with less drama than the first time, courtesy of a momentary lull in the storm.

Jack and Hamlin had the lighthouse keeper on the stretcher and his wife aboard in seconds.

Jack didn't risk coming around the front of the helo but instead entered by the cargo bay and climbed over the radio console, dripping water everywhere, to get to his seat. She didn't look at him, she was far too intent on what might be flying her way next.

"Let's go, Wonder Woman."

She waited on the wind and then jerked aloft in the midst of a strong gust that would give her a lot of lift.

With a patient to work on, the medic was done cursing his ankle. Hamlin was still talking down the near-panicked wife.

"He's responding well," the medic reported.

Diana could hear a machine now beeping in the background.

"We need to get him to a hospital, but the wife is requesting Seattle and he'll be good for that long."

"Roger," Diana acknowledged, then she switched off the intercom to the rear of the helo.

Instead of turning for Seattle, she took one more pass out over the beach.

"What is it?" Jack looked like a drowned rat, a big, very handsome one.

She'd never been so happy to see anyone in her life. It had finally sunk in that because she'd flown away from the lighthouse without telling him why, that a ghost net could ensnare him and drag him away into the permanent darkness.

Another lesson, okay to leave the ground, but don't leave your team without a warning.

She nodded forward and down, "Look."

"Nothing on infrared or radar," he began working the radio.

Then she spotted it in the first faint hint of dawn beyond the black clouds. A forty-footer, belly up. Caught in the shallows well off the spit.

She quartered the waves several times, but there was no one there. A final pass along the beach, no one in the surf or washed up. It would be a grim job for the Coast Guard after the storm died.

Jack called it in and she turned for Seattle, climbing and laying down the hammer.

"Dead," Diana swallowed hard and tried not to think of her father. "That fast."

"I know. Nothing we can do to help them."

She slewed past Port Townsend and turned south for Seattle. "That's not the point."

Jack gave her his attention, another thing to like about him.

Into that silence she spilled out her past, or more accurately her mother's. A man beloved and then dead. All that he'd left behind had been a child and a woman's heart so full of love that there had never been room for another. She'd dated, but never loved again.

"You really believe that?" he asked it softly.

"What?"

"That a heart can do that? That one person can fill it for a lifetime?"

Diana could hear the deeper question behind it, even if she didn't know the details.

"Better than believe. I've seen it. If you were to meet Mom, you'd see it too. It shines out of her."

His silence was different this time, though no less deep.

She had to handle the radio calls to Harborview Medical Center Heliport in Seattle. The winds were mostly at thirty knots and dropping, she could land well enough in that. The morning's light was slowly revealing the city—the perimeter lights on the helipad were barely needed anymore.

They off-loaded the man and his wife to the waiting med team. The medic decided his own injury was a sprain, so he stayed on board to deal with it at Lewis-McChord.

They were aloft again for the short flight back to base before Jack spoke again.

"I have no experience with anything lasting. The only thing that's ever lasted in my entire life has been flying for the Army."

This time it was her turn to remain silent.

"But what you make me feel, Wonder Woman," and she could hear the joy back in his voice, that joy that had radiated from him since the moment she'd first met Jack-the-Giant-Killer.

Oh god how she wanted to be a part of that joy.

"I don't have the words for it though I spent all last night looking for them. Whatever it is, I want to feel that every single day of my life."

All she could think to whisper was, "Me too."

She kept her right hand on the cyclic, but moved her left one off the collective.

He did the opposite, keeping control of the collective with his left. Between them, their outside hands had control of the aircraft.

They finished the flight back home, flying together through the quieting storm over the terrain glistening in the first rays of sunlight.

And holding each other's inside hands tightly as they flew.

About the Author

M. L. Buchman has over 30 novels in print. His military romantic suspense books have been named Barnes & Noble and NPR "Top 5 of the year" and Booklist "Top 10 of the Year." In addition to romance, he also writes thrillers, fantasy, and science fiction.

In among his career as a corporate project manager he has: rebuilt and single-handed a fifty-foot sailboat, both flown and jumped out of airplanes, designed and built two houses, and bicycled solo around the world. He is now making his living as a full-time writer on the Oregon Coast with his beloved wife. He is constantly amazed at what you can do with a degree in Geophysics. You may keep up with his writing by subscribing to his newsletter at

www.mlbuchman.com.

Target of the Heart

-a new Night Stalkers team-
(excerpt)

Major Pete Napier hovered his MH-60M Black hawk helicopter ten kilometers outside of Lhasa, Tibet and two inches off the tundra. A mixed action team of Delta Force and The Activity—the slipperiest intel group on the planet—piled aboard from both sides.

The rear cabin doors slid home with a *Thunk! Thunk!* that sent a vibration through his pilot's seat and an infinitesimal shift in the cyclic control in his right hand. By the time his crew chief could reach forward to slap an "all secure" signal against his shoulder, they were already fifty feet out and ten up. That was enough altitude. He kept the nose down as he clawed for speed in the thin air at eleven thousand feet.

"Totally worth it," one of the D-boys announced as soon as he was on the intercom.

"Great, now I just need to get us out of this alive."

"Do that, Pete. We'd appreciate it."

He wished to hell he had a stealth bird like the one that had gone into bin Laden's compound. But the one that had crashed during that raid had been blown up. Where there was one, there were always two, but the second had gone back into hiding as thoroughly as if it had never existed. He hadn't heard a word about it since.

It was amazing, the largest city in Tibet and ten kilometers away equaled barren wilderness. He could crash out here and no one would know for decades unless some Yak herder stumbled upon them. Or was Yaks Mongolia? He was a dark-haired, corn-fed, white boy from Colorado, what did he know about Tibet? Most of the countries he'd flown into on black ops missions he'd only seen at night while moving very, very fast. Like now.

The inside of his visor was painted with overlapping readouts. A pre-defined terrain map, the best that modern satellite imaging could build made the first layer. This wasn't some crappy, on-line, look-at-a-picture-of-your-house display. Someone had a pile of dung outside their goat pen? He could see it, tell you how high it was, and probably say if they were pygmy goats or full-size LaManchas by the size of their shit-pellets.

On top of that was projected the forward-looking infrared camera images. The FLIR imaging gave him a real-time overlay, in case someone had put an addition onto their goat house since the last satellite pass, or parked their tractor across his intended flight path.

His nervous system was paying auto-
nomic attention to that combined landscape.
He was automatically compensating for
the thin air at altitude as he instinctively
chose when to start his climb over said goat
house or his swerve around it.

It was the third layer, the tactical display
that had most of his attention. To insert
this deep into Tibet, without passing over
Bhutan or Nepal, they'd had to add wing-
tanks on the helicopter's hardpoints where
he'd much rather have a couple banks of
Hellfire missiles.

At least he and the two Black Hawks
flying wingman on him were finally on the
move.

While the action team was busy infiltrating
the capital city and gathering intelligence
on the particularly brutal Chinese assistant
administrator, he and his crews had been
squatting out in the wilderness under
a camouflage net designed to make his
helo look like just another god-forsaken
Himalayan lump of granite.

Command had determined that it was
better to wait through the day than risk

flying out and back in. He and his crew had stood shifts on guard duty, but none of them had slept. They'd been flying together too long to have any new jokes, so they'd played a lot of cribbage. He'd long ago ruled no gambling on deployment after a fistfight had broken out over a bluff that cost a Marine over three hundred dollars. Marines hated losing to Army. They'd had to sit on him for a long time before he calmed down.

Tonight's mission was part of an on-going campaign to discredit the Chinese "presence" in Tibet on the international stage—as if occupying the country the last sixty years didn't count toward ruling, whether invited or not. As usual, there was a crucial vote coming up at the U.N.—that, as usual, the Chinese could be guaranteed to ignore. However, the ever-hopeful CIA was in a hurry to make sure that any damaging information that they could validate was disseminated as thoroughly as possible prior to the vote.

Not his concern. His concern was, were they going to pass over some Chinese sentry post at just under two hundred miles an hour? The sentries would then call down a couple Shenyang J-16 jet fighters that could hustle along at Mach 2 to fry his sorry ass. He knew there was a pair of them parked at Lhasa along with some older gear that would be just as effective against his three helos.

"Don't suppose you could get a move on, Pete?"

"Eat shit, Nicolai!" He was a good man to have as a copilot. Pete knew he was holding on too tight, and Nicolai knew that a joke was the right way to ease the moment.

He, Nicolai, and his fellow pilots had a long way to go tonight. They dove down into gorges and followed them as long as they dared. They hugged cliff walls at every opportunity to decrease their radar profile. And they climbed.

That was the true danger—they would be up near the Black Hawks' limits when they crossed over the backbone of the Himalayas in their rush for India. The air was so rarefied that they burned fuel at a prodigious rate. Their reserve didn't allow for any extended battles while crossing the border…not for any battle at all really.

# # #

It was pitch dark outside her helicopter when Captain Danielle Delacroix stamped on the left rudder pedal while giving the Black Hawk right control on cyclic. It tipped her most of the way onto her side, but let her continue in a straight line. A Black Hawk's rotor was fifty-four feet across. By cross-controlling her bird to tip it, she managed to execute a straight line between two pylons only thirty feet apart.

At her current angle of attack, she took up less than a half-rotor of width, twenty-four feet. That left her three feet to either side, sufficient as she was moving at under a hundred knots.

The training instructor sitting beside her in the copilot's seat didn't react as she swooped through the training course in Fort Campbell, Kentucky.

After two years of training with the U.S. Army's 160th Special Operations

Aviation Regiment, she was ready for some action. At least she was convinced that she was. But the trainers of Fort Campbell, Kentucky had not signed off on her class yet. Nor had they given any hint of when they might.

She ducked under a bridge and bounced into a near vertical climb to clear the power line on the far side. Like a ride at *le carnaval,* only with five thousand horsepower.

To even apply to SOAR required five years of prior military rotorcraft experience. She had applied because of a chance encounter—or rather what she'd thought was a chance encounter at the time.

Captain Justin Roberts had been a top Chinook pilot, the one who had convinced her to cross-train from her beloved Black Hawk and try out the massive twin-rotor craft. He'd made the jump from the 10th Mountain Division to the 160th SOAR after he'd been in the service for five years.

Then one night she'd been having pizza in Watertown, New York a couple miles off the 10th's base at Fort Drum. Justin had greeted her with surprise and shared her pizza. Had said he was just in town visiting old haunts. Her questions had naturally led to discussions of his experiences at SOAR. He'd even paid for the pizza after eating half.

He'd left her interested enough to fill out an application to the 160th. The speed at which she was rushed into testing told her that her meeting with Justin hadn't been by chance and that she owed him more than half a pizza next time they met. She'd asked around once she'd passed the qualification exams and a brutal set of interviews that had left her questioning her sanity, never mind her ability. "Justin Roberts is presently deployed, ma'am," was the only response she'd ever gotten.

The training course was never the same, but it always had a time limit. The time would be short and they didn't tell you what it was. So she drove the Black Hawk for all it was worth like Regina Jaquess waterskiing her way to U.S. Ski Team female athlete of the year.

The Night Stalkers were a damned secretive lot, and after two years of training, she understood why. With seven years flying for the 10th, she'd thought she was good.

She'd been one of the top pilots at Fort Drum.

The Night Stalkers had offered an education in what it really meant to fly. In the two years of training, she'd flown more hours than in the seven years prior, despite two deployments to Iraq. And spent more time in the classroom than her life-to-date accumulated flight hours.

But she was ready now. It was *très viscérale,* right down in her bones she could feel it. The Black Hawk was as much a part of her nervous system as breathing. As were the Little Bird and the massive Chinook.

She dove down into a canyon and slid to a hover mere inches over the reservoir inside the thirty-second window laid out on the flight plan.

Danielle resisted a sigh. She was ready for something to happen and to happen soon.

#

Pete Napier and his two fellow Black Hawks crossed into the mountainous province of Sikkim, India ten feet over the glaciers and still moving fast. It was an hour before dawn.

"Twenty minutes of fuel remaining," Nicolai said it like personal challenge when they hit the border.

"Thanks, I never would have noticed."

It had been a nail-biting tradeoff: the more fuel he burned, the more easily he climbed due to the lighter load. The more he climbed, the faster he burned what little fuel remained.

He climbed hard as Nicolai counted down the minutes remaining, burning fuel even faster than he had been crossing the mountains of southern Tibet. They caught up with the U.S. Air Force HC-130P Combat King refueling tanker with only ten minutes of fuel left.

"Ram that bitch."

Pete extended the refueling probe which extended beyond the forward edge of the rotor blade and drove at the basket trailing behind the tanker on its long hose.

He nailed it on the first try despite the fluky winds.

"Ah," Nicolai sighed. "It is better than the sex," his thick Russian accent only ever surfaced in this moment or in a bar while picking up women.

His helo had the least fuel due to having the most men aboard, so he was first in line. His Number Two picked up the second refueling basket trailing off the other wing of the HC-130P. A quick five hundred gallons and he was breathing much more easily.

Another two hours of—thank god—straight and level flight at altitude, and they arrived at the aircraft carrier awaiting them in the Bay of Bengal. India had agreed to turn a blind eye as long as the Americans never actually touched their soil.

Once out on deck—and the worst of the kinks worked out—he pulled his team together, six pilots and six crew chiefs.

"Honor to serve!" He saluted them sharply.

"Hell yeah!" They shouted in response and saluted in turn. It their version of spiking the football in the end zone.

A petty officer in a bright green vest appeared at his elbow, "Follow me please, sir." He pointed toward the Navy-gray command structure that towered above the carrier's deck. The Commodore of the entire carrier group was waiting for him just outside the entrance.

The green escorted him across the hazards of the busy flight deck. Pete pulled his helmet on to buffer the noise of an F-18 Hornet firing up and being flung off the catapult.

"Orders, Major Napier," the Commodore handed him a folded sheet. "Hate to lose you."

The Commodore saluted, which Pete automatically returned before looking down at the sheet of paper in his hands. The man was gone before the import of Pete's orders slammed in.

A different green showed up with his duffle and began guiding him toward a loading C-2 Greyhound twin prop airplane. It was parked number two for the launch catapult, close behind the raised jet-blast deflector.

What in the name of fuck-all had he done to deserve this?

He glanced at the orders again as he stumbled up the Greyhound's rear ramp and crash landed into a seat.

Training rookies?

It was worse than a demotion.

This was punishment.

***

Available at fine retailers everywhere

More information at:
www.mlbuchman.com

/

Printed in Great Britain
by Amazon